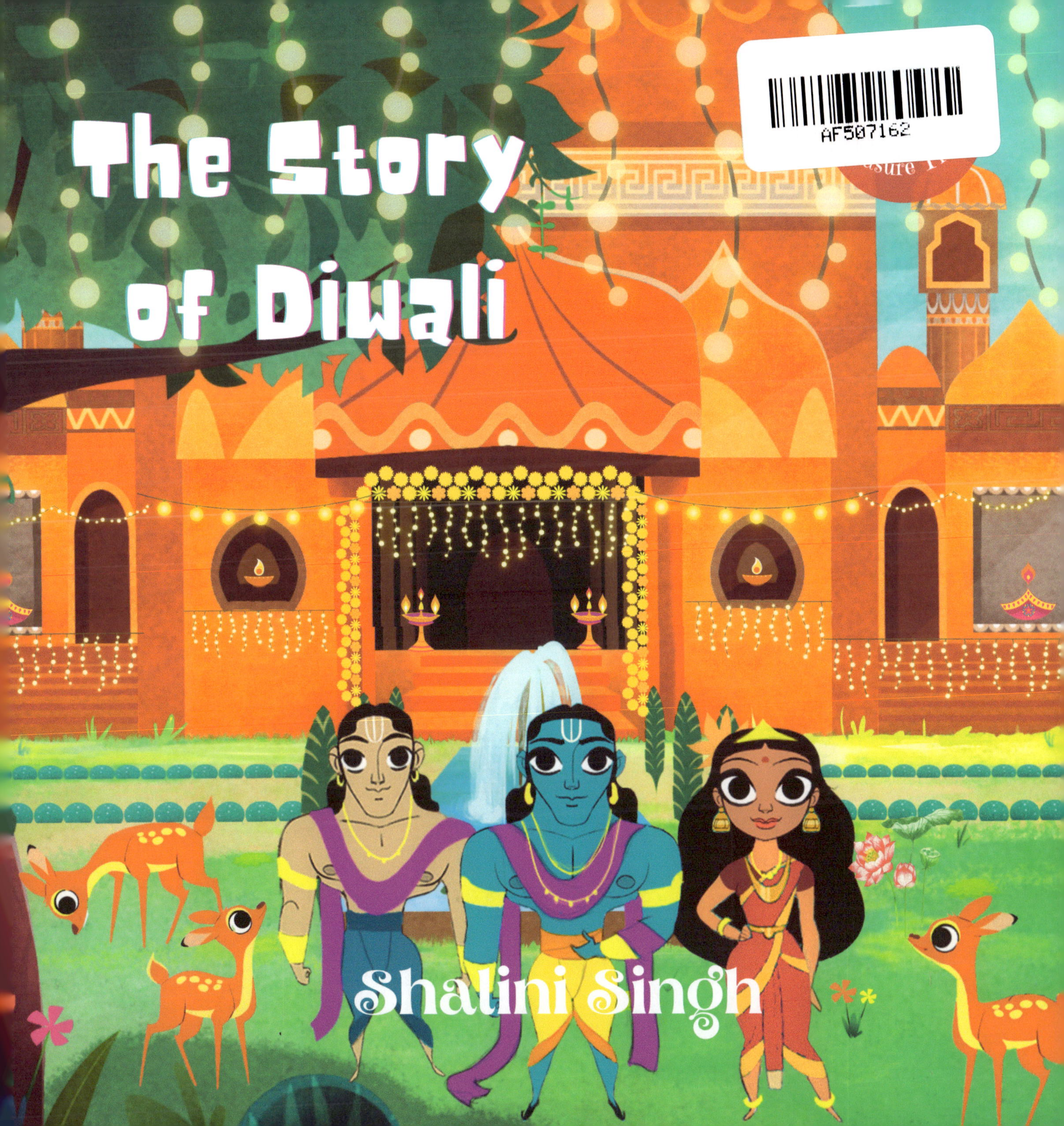

The Story
of Diwali
Shalini Singh

This Book belongs to

....

First paperback edition September 2022

Published by Amazon Kdp & Notion Press

India is a beautiful land of diversity
and celebrates many, many festivals.
Have you ever heard of the
Festival of Lights?
Yes! you're right! It's called Diwali!
Now, this festival is celebrated
in honour of Good over Evil.
But, do you know, there is a thrilling story
behind this festival?
Come, let's find out more...

In the peaceful city of Ayodhya, there brewed a sinister plot that would change the face of history forever...

Within the massive walls of the palace, the
King of Ayodhya, Dashrath, lived with his 3 wives.
The first wife, Kausalya's son was Ram, who also lived in
this palace, with Sita, his beautiful wife and his younger
brother Lakshman.
However, the second wife of the King, named Kaikeyi
was quite jealous and wanted her own son Bharath, to
become the King, even though Ram was the rightful heir to
the throne.

Many years ago, when King Dashrath fell into bad times, it was Queen Kaikeyi who had helped him. In return, she had made the King promise, that he would grant her ONE wish of whatever she desired, without questioning her.

Now the time had come, for Ram's coronation. This was the opportune time, Kaikeyi had chosen to get King Dashrath, to grant her the wish, that he had promised.

Evil Kaikeyi, commanded poor King Dashrath, to banish his
son Ram into exile, by sending him into the forest, for 14
years. It was her evil plan, to crown her own son Bharath,
and make him the King of Ayodhya, instead of Ram.
Meanwhile, Ram's wife Sita and his brother Lakshman,
refused to let Ram go alone and therefore, the three of
them set off into the depths of the forest,
much to the dismay and sadness of the people of Ayodhya.

In the forest, an evil demon princess Surpanakha,
was watching Ram everyday and fell in love with him.
She turned herself into a beautiful woman and
approached him to marry her.
Ram told her that he was already married to Sita.

She then approached Lakshman and asked HIM to marry her, but he too refused!
She was enraged and changed herself back into a demon, to fight Lakshman for refusing to marry her.
Lakshman fought back and cut off her nose!

Wailing loudly, Surpanakha ran to complain to her
brother, who was none other than,
the evil King of Lanka, Ravan!
Ravan was furious, and plotted to take revenge on
Ram and Lakshman.

He stepped into his Flying Chariot, the
Pushpaka Vimana and headed for the
Dandaka forest with a vengeance.

While Ram and Lakshman were walking deep into the forest, they spotted a beautiful Golden deer and started following it with curiosity. Actually, the deer was a demon, who was sent by the terrible Ravan, to distract the brothers, Ram and Lakshman.

This demon was called Mareechan, who was capable of changing his shape whenever he wanted. Ravan used this opportunity, since he knew Sita was all alone and it was very easy to capture her.

Ravan captured Sita and whisked her away to Lanka, in his flying chariot, where he kept her captive.

Jatayu the vulture friend of King Dashrath, tried stopping Ravan, but was injured badly and only lived long enough to tell Ram of Sita's kidnapping.

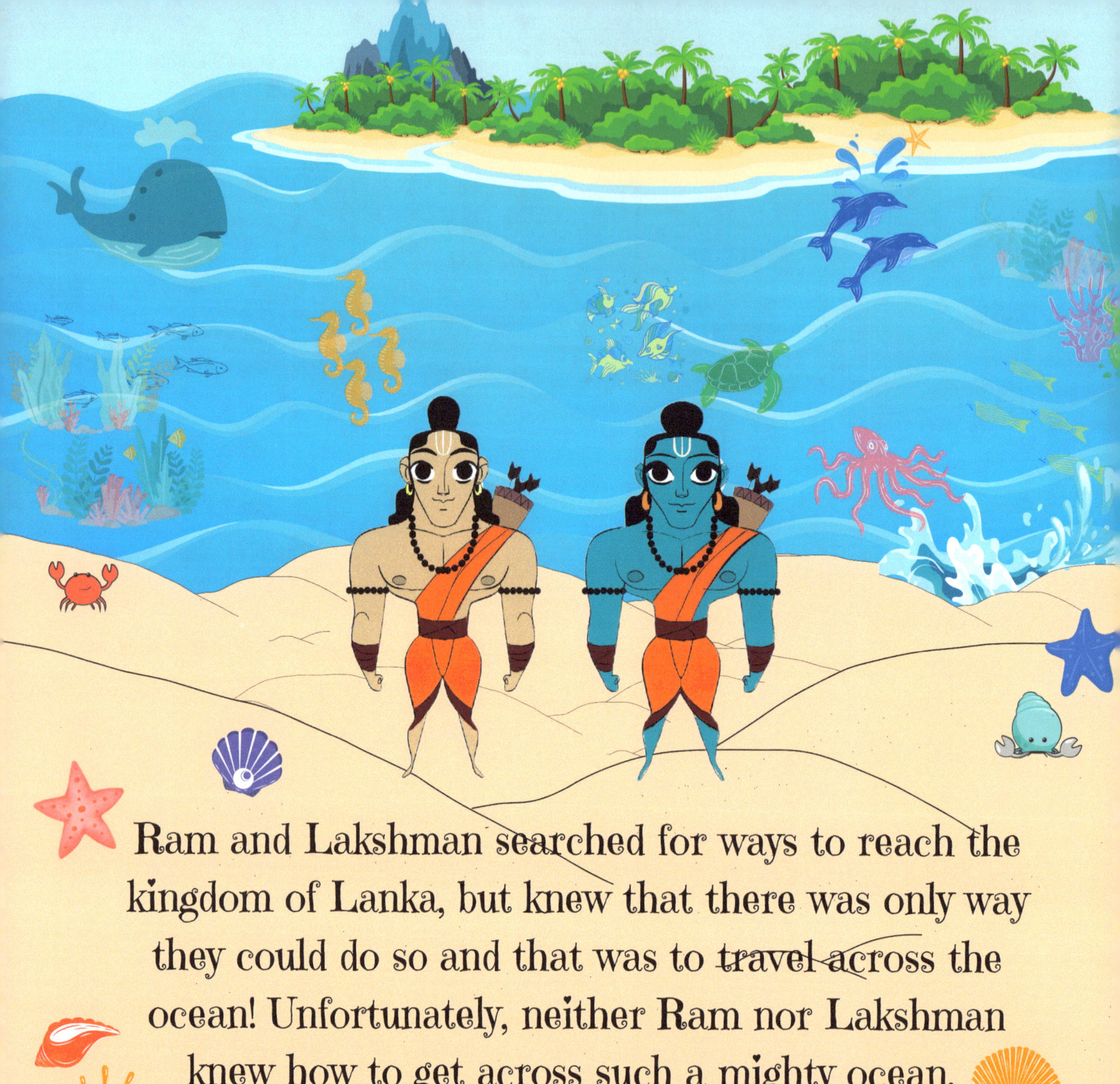

Ram and Lakshman searched for ways to reach the kingdom of Lanka, but knew that there was only way they could do so and that was to travel across the ocean! Unfortunately, neither Ram nor Lakshman knew how to get across such a mighty ocean.

While on their way, they had helped the monkey King Sugreeva to regain his position and he in return promised to help them find Sita.

Sugreeva had an army of monkeys and leading this army was the flying monkey Hanuman.

Hanuman flew across the ocean and found Sita in King Ravan's palace garden. Sita was so happy that Ram was coming to rescue her.

She gives Hanuman her ring and asks him to take this token of her love and give it to Ram. Hanuman took the ring and promised to return with Ram and his army to rescue her.

The army of monkeys, created a bridge of stones across the ocean and charged ahead to the kingdom of Lanka.

On reaching Lanka, Ram requested Ravan, one last time, to release Sita. But Ravan, stubbornly refused to do so and that's when a fierce battle began.

Ravan's army tried setting fire to Hanuman's tail,
but he in return used that fire to set ablaze the
entire kingdom of Lanka.

But even this did not stop Ravan from relentlessly
fighting Ram.
The people of Lanka ran helter - skelter in fear of their
lives, but yet their king Ravan did not bother at all.

Seeing the devastation all around him, Ram was deeply saddened and prayed to the thousand - eyed Lord Indra to help him.

Lord Indra heard his prayer and bestowed on him the powerful Brahmastra. Ram placed the Brahmastra on his bow and aimed the arrow directly at Ravan.

Thunder struck and the Earth shook, as the Brahmastra flew swiftly through the air and finally pierced through the heart of the merciless ten-headed Ravan, killing him instantly. This was the historical battle of Ram's victory over Ravan, or which is commonly known as the victory of Good over Evil.

14 years had passed by and it was time for Ram to return to
Ayodhya.
The entire city of Ayodhya was lit up with a million lights, in
wait for their beloved Ram.
As Ram entered the city of Ayodhya, everybody shouted in joy
and lit up the sky with sparkling fireworks.
Since then Diwali has been celebrated, as the mark of Good
over Evil and Ram's victorious return to Ayodhya.

HAPPY
DIWALI

SITA

COLOURING PAGE
RAMA

Thank you for reading
'**The Story of Diwali**'
If you liked this book,
do leave your reviews and feedback.
Would love to hear from you! ❤

Also check out my other book!

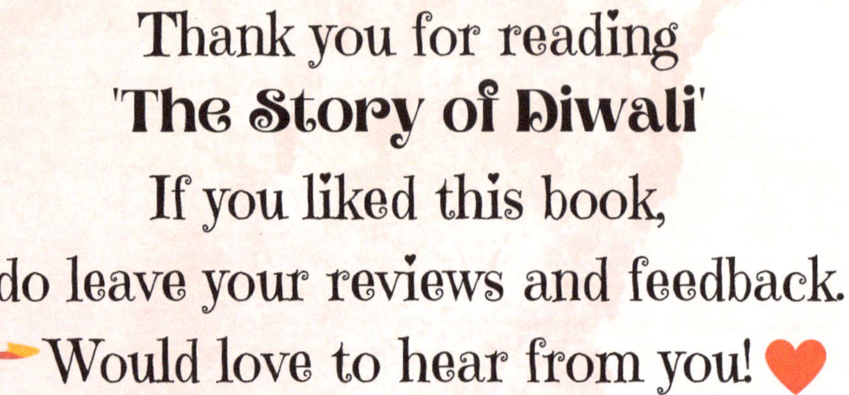

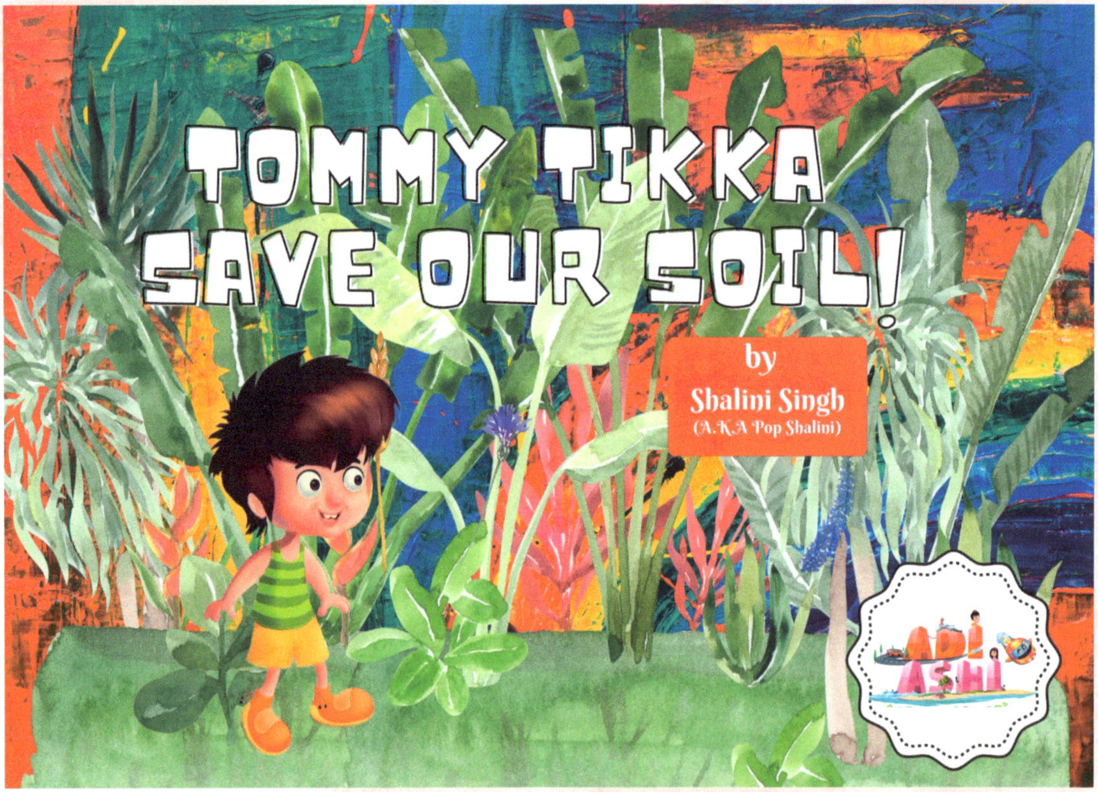